Sometimes, when she smoked, I used to light it up for her.

She would say –

"you are not going to do it for long".

I used to say – "I can do it for life-long".

She

would reply and say – "we will see"…

A DEBUT NOVEL

With gripping narrative of the night and its' slow burn nature...there were tales to be told and tales to be forgotten.

Even if u can't predict the future, you can certainly smell the essence of it. What its' going to look-like and where can I fit in those (these) elements. Just a minute, this lamp belongs here, and I am going to keep this door mate in this room and so on!

This is what we do and we love to, because here we have a freedom to move things or to get things done according to our needs. Its' a floating world and we let ourselves float in it, and we do feel light, light like air; but here, not air, who has command (control) over our swing of directions. Its' us, its' always been us here.

1

VIRANG

It was 10 past 9 at night. A foggy storm seemed to be arriving from the dark corner of the road. When I smoked the cigarette, I was unable to find out that whether the smoke was from it or it was just that I was smoking the fog. I arrived here to work for an advertising agency and to some extent get back to a normal life and out of the past blurs.

I was allotted an out of the town modernly build house by the company's agent. As I moved in, I realized there were not many nieghbours to talk to and also to get the supplies I had to kind of go to the town part of the city.

When I returned after my introduction day from the work, I found a girl at my garden looking to jump over the fence. She said she has lost her skateboard while skating. I was confused whether a skate can go that far to be lost.

She introduced herself as 'Anna' and said she moved here to be a writer and said she wants to write something out of this world. With no offence, when I said you could have done that by staying at home with her parents. She nodded and said that she couldn't find the peace that she wanted there.

She asked my name, I told her its' 'Virang'. She smiled and said, well 'Virang' I will see u soon again. I replied yeah, not by climbing over my fence. She chuckled, and said definitely not and pointed her finger towards a nearby home and said won't mind if you need anything since there are only a few houses around.

Few days passed, we seem to get along well. One day I asked her if she does not mind I would like to help her with her writing through my advertising agency to give her the required uplift in her carrier. She asked, but how? I said I could pursue my boss to run an ad campaign seeking out young authors and liking it to our social cause related programs. She was quite happy with the whole idea.

One day she asked me that where exactly I lived before I got here. Normally someone would ask that question on the first meet, I said well, actually I lived in the same city as I am now, its' just I lived in the town part of the city. She said why someone would move here from a good and modern life. I just smiled and said well sometimes you need a change and you needed peace for your writing, maybe I need something else from this place.

After a while she completed her first book and I took her book for my company's showcase program. Everything went well and she was eventually selected as one of the entrants whom the agency decided to sponsor.

After a few weeks, i asked her out, we went for a lunch at the town. On our way to return we came across a huge house cum villa.

I stopped and I couldn't help myself but kept looking at it as if I knew it before or lived there before. Anna noticed the sadness in my eyes. She didn't asked anything for the rest of the way, but when we returned, she said Virang – "I want to know everything about what happened today or

whether you have anything to do with that place"..?
Next weekend I took her to that house.

Her eyes were amazed as probably she had never
seen something that beautiful before. As she was
looking around I just sat on of the garden stairs and
started crying. I didn't want her to hear me but
when I turned she was standing right behind me.
She sat with me and said "you need to tell me
everything Virang". I wiped my tears and said,
"something happened when I lived here",
"something really bad".

I told her I would tell her everything about my past,
but first we should return back to my house and
away from the town. She agreed.

When we got back I started telling her about what
happened ....

I moved to that house, my father's house which my
elder Brother-'Ayan'..inherited from him after his
death, but I was wasn't alone. I got there with my
girlfriend. Her name was 'Neha'. We were quite
new in our relationship and we were still getting to
know each other. I liked her, the way she was.

Everything was moving really well. Just like you, she also loved the house. As I decided to spend more time with my agency she took a break and decided to decorate the house interiors according to her much wished preferences. I agreed as I thought she would probably get accustomed to the house and more to the people around her.

I got distracted from my work and from our relationship, I didn't knew when but when one of my collegemates 'Kaya' moved in my agency as an HR, we got close. Most of the times due to work related matters, We bonded well. One of my colleauges ("Ronin") didn't liked our closeness and he was not that good to me. I guess he liked 'Kaya'.

There was a party at the bosses home. I asked 'Neha' to join us but she refused and said to me she had other plans for the weekend and moreover I guess she was happy following her long driven passion for interior designing. I said I would like to have a say in it as well. She laughed and said – of course.

I went to the party. Kaya was there. Ronin was there too. It was almost inevitable to talk about the love which was in the eyes of Kaya for those little moments that we spent together. She has got that little sparkle about her from our college days. I guess that's what attracted me towards her sometimes.

We were sitting in a room of our Boss's house. We were talking about our old days. Certainly there was only me and Kaya in the room as everyone went out to get themselves a drink or another. Kaya started to laugh on a joke and she splited her drink on her dress. As I leaned to help her out with my handkerchief, we had a little moment. We kissed and I stopped hesitantly for a moment, but she persisted softly and looked me in my eyes..and we went on.

I guess Ronin was just getting back after getting a drink. He spotted the opportunity to spoil my everything by using that moment. He clicked our pictures in his mobile phone.

He (Ronin) sented those pictures to 'Neha'. Neha after seeing those pictures was just completely broken I guess, or she must have taken her car and decided to leave without saying a word to me or maybe she decided to storm into the party for probably a justification from me. She probably didn't made it, wherever she was headed to, in that cold weather of that night. She met an accident.

A harsh one, and she was gone, just like that. It appeared that in the blink of an eye, everything turned that way.

After that I had tried to comeback to this house many times and wanted to live my life in the sameway as was before, but it was without 'Neha'. I tried so hard, but every corner of the house has her smell, the way she decorated it. The more I wanted to forget her..the more the house was dragging me towards her.

At last I realized I couldn't take it anymore at this house. It had to be a fresh start for me to get myself out in the world and get back on track. Ronin lefted the Country after the accident when I came to knew about his whereabouts.

Going after him wouldn't have brought back 'Neha' for me. Kaya tried to help me out by talking me through that period but I guess she realized - I was not the same as I was before. Everything kind of changed after Neha. Kaya also knew that deep inside I would never forgive that moment between us that lead to everything afterwards.

She (Kaya) knew I must be blaming our friendship for the reason to loose Neha and not only the relationship but to loose her from this world.

2

ANNA

No matter what we did, Virang was never very happy and lively. I guess after telling all that story to me.. he was again more lost inside his past than he was before. I feel as if his mind was here but his heart and soul was in that house. "If something could kill you and make you live at the same time"...I guess that thing for Virang was that house.

When we often use to go to city for a day-or-two, he would usually stop his car and would light up his cigarette and would keep looking at the house for a long time. I just couldn't figure out whether he wants his previous life with Neha back or he just needs his time to flush out those memories.

I had fallen for him and deep inside I knew, he likes me too. I just want to be with him and I don't know where this all will take me , but **"sometimes we are better off choosing the road that has an uncertain**

distance to an end than to choose an end that we are uncertain with".

I pursued Virang to move into that house for somedays if not forever or a long time.

 I knew it will be hard to convince him but anything that could make him live again was that house, but I also knew it could kill him once again in such a way that I might not be able to get him back from it. He said no at first but after few days he came to me and said, he wants to do it.

Virang seemed a lot more interested in his works than he was before. I was happy for him. One day he asked me 'Anna' "would you mind if I show you a closet which had different clothes that belonged to Neha". Virang said he wasn't able to figure out which one to keep and if he should leave it as it was and it was hard for him to see all those stuff again.

When Virang was gone for work – I was having a look into the old things from that closet, I found a strange note lying in one of the drawers it had. It said – " *I Want to Love You More, but I Can't*". I wonder if that was written by 'Neha'.

I didn't wanted to discuss anything about it with Virang as it might disrupt the way he's been feeling lately. I had nobody else to talk to regarding the matter. So, I decided to keep it to myself for the time being.

One day, when I was watering the plants in the garden, the very garden where Virang sat and told me about his past. Suddenly a girl dressed in a black type coat showed up. She looked like "as if an angel was wearing the devil's clothes".

I asked her - I wonder how you got in, do I know you..?, I must have forgot to lock the doors. She replied – "You must have, or you must have locked it so tightly, that the people who were already in, can't find a way out.

I said – "who are you"..?

She replied in a deep mysterious voice and said, "You must ask this question to yourself and your love", "don't you want to know more about him..? You know, It's not often what we see, it's more of what we don't".

As I turned away in anger and with a slight egoist laugh said that – " I know him more than he himself does". And then when I turned back to say a few more things – there was no one there – as if I was talking to myself. I searched everywhere in the house, but there was no one inside and more so the door was locked.

The incident shooked me to the extent, I started to think that I must be hallucinating or something, or I must be thinking to much about all the things that happened in the last month or so, all the things that 'Virang' told me about.

I decided to call my mother – and I told her few of the things that happened lately, and she suggested – I better take a break and come back to her for a few days and my mind of rest of the things. I didn't tell her anything about Virang. I guessed it was too deep a hole to be filled over a phone call.

I told her I would think about it, but in the back of my mind, I had already decided that I would stay here with Virang as much as I can and would try to find out whatever I can and yes, just like about that note that I found in the Closet, I also did not tell Virang anything about that Garden incident with that stranger girl.

I knew I should tell him, but it was hard for me to involve him in another mess, (and that too, possibly in a mess that was mine) after what he has been through.

I decided to meet 'Kaya' and see if she can tell me something about Virang's past, which was maybe hidden from me or which Virang did not told me. Also I decided that I would tell her about the incident at the house which has me on the edge from the past few days.

I told Virang that one of my old friend just had a breakup recently and she has not been feeling good lately, so she wants me to come over for a few days and it's just a couple of hours journey from here. Virang said ok and he insisted me to take my time off as it had been quite a few days since I went out.

3

VIRANG

'Anna' has been my life after 'Neha'. She is indeed the reason for me to be alive. But what she doesn't know is that I am not completely out of the trauma which I had been struck with and everything is not the way it seems to be. Maybe she does not know me all or may be she knows me better than me.

There are reasons for my actions. Anna might have seen something or heard somethings from me about my past but may be theirs' more to know about that.

As I get through my daily life, I notice a secretive anxiety in the Anna's eyes, as if she wants to know something which either didn't happened or wasn't supposed to have happened.

I know she's not the type of person to hold back. But I also want her to search her own answers, or maybe I don't want to listen to her questions.

4

ANNA & KAYA

I went to Kaya. She started living in a different place. I guess everybody needed a change after that incident.

I asked her about Virang and if he had told her something about him and Neha's relationship that was only between them.

She said that she would tell me everything and there's a reason for that. As she cared for Virang and wanted him to be happy and said she knows that now if there's a person that would be with him and look after him, that would be me.

She said – last winter Virang told me something very odd about his relationship with Neha. It was in the middle of the night that he arrived at my house and said that he wanted to tell me something. I said ok, but will you speak, because he was rather shivering and was not saying anything.

He said not everything is well between him and Neha. He also said that – Neha seems upset a lot of times and it's like she wants to say or ask something from me but she can't. She almost muffers first words of a sentence, but than she stops.

It's like she's keeping something from me and I can't get it out of her and he said that he feels very numb about it and it bothers him to an extent that he can't focus on anything else.

He seemed shaken to an extent that would need some consoling to be done. But you know Anna, my mother used to say – **"there's always a reason why we can't find the last piece of a puzzle, it's because we often put that first one wrong"**.

After that night, whe Virang left, I called Ronin and came to knew that Neha's health has been not that well lately, and Virang has been missing a lot of workdays also.

It took me time as I decided to dig deep but after sometime I came to knew that – " I and Neha were not the only girls that Virang had seen over the last year or so. I came to know it from one of Virang's friend who Virang introduced to me at a bar. The Oldman (Francis) told me these and said that he would tell me the things that he knows about Virang's past, after I persuaded him a lot.

The Oldman (Francis) called me to his house on next Saturday. I said ok, I will be there.

When I reached his house, he told me that Virang was with a girl before he met Neha and according to him they seemed to be more than just friends.

He told me that – he met Virang through Virang's elder brother. Whenever they meet Virang used to mention about that girl. He seemed to be very consumed with her. There was a great sparkle in his eyes whenever he talked about her. But he never used to take her name and mention any other details about her, he was very secretive towards any such talk.

Francis also said – There was always something about him (Virang) that will instigate you to know him more. Somedays he seemed to be very happy and would talk about his personal life also. While the very next when we will meet in a bar or so, he would be very quiet and reserve, as if he wants to hide something and thinks that if he interacts he might give away something that he should not.

Anna, I think you should ask 'Virang' about all these, to know if his hiding something, before it's too late. To love a person whom you don't know completely can almost end up hurting you. I feel, **What he's been through and what he's is going through and hiding underneath himself, you must know that, before there's nothing left to be known**.

5

ANNA

When I came back home – Virang had just came back from work. After we had dinner, he asked me that if something happened today (and that I look a bit tensed). I hesitated for that moment but then I decided that I would say to Virang that I want to ask him about somethings. And if not today perhaps he could answer my questions tomorrow after returning from work in the evening.

There was a turmoil going within me, I was shivering inside, whatever I had came to knew today, has shaken me uo and I just wonder what lies ahead and whether Virang would open up to me or not.

As much as I knew him, yes there are things that he keeps from me, but I guess, if he tells me everything, I just wished that everything between us stays and my love for him doesn't get hurt.

" If today came closer to revealing the story, I just wished that tomorrow must not end it ".

The next evening came, and when Virang was sitting on the couch after returning from work, I went there and sat in front of him, he kept the stuff down which he was reading and said to me – "you wanted to ask me something", "what was it..?, you can ask it now".

I asked him – "what is it that he is hiding from me, what is that bothers you but you can't tell me"..?.."Let it bother me first, let it keep me quiet, not you". "I will suffer your pain, I will suffer your loss".

I went to Kaya and asked her about you. I asked her that if there's anything that you have told her about your past that I don't know. She told me the things that Francis (The Oldman) one of your friends' told her about you. Things that are important about your past, things that are important to know you.

Their has been weird things happening in this house. I found a note in that closet which you told me to look after, as it was hard for you to do so. It was written in the note that – " *I Want to Love You More, but I Can't* ". Why would someone write something like that – You tell me Virang. And than another day there's a girl that walked into our garden and told me that – "I don't know everything about you". How did she got in..? I have nevere seen her before. I checked the fucking doors, they were locked.

After all that you and I had been through, how can someone come in our house and say things lioke that to me about you. I have not seen her since then, anywhere near our house. Nobody seems to know her here, when I describe her appearance to them. I think I must have been thinking too much or it must have been a day dream or an illusion." *You tell me Virang, in this quest of finding you...am I loosing myself"..?*

I may have over thought the things, about you, about whatever you told me about you and Neha, the way things ended between you. After we have moved into this house, all I wanted is you to be happy. But it seems to me like – everything is fucking-up my mind..it's just all blowing in my face and sometimes I think, I have started seeing things, but that's not the case, as it was as real as it gets, whatever I saw was real, that moment was real enough to be true.

I never told you anything about all of these as I knew you just got out of your loss of Neha, we had just started to live our life. you have started to talk more and I don't wanted to throw you in all those mess which I even don't know how to explain to myself. I thought I would find the answers myself and I did, but only to some extent, and I believe there is more to it, there always has been.

6

VIRANG

It was before the last winter, when I just used to visit my elder brother – "Ayan" on weekdays. This house was in his name. We used to spent weekends together playing Tennis and having conservations on different work related topics. This was such a big house, as it is now along with the garden lawns that he said it used to get awkward on the weekends to stay there alone, he told me that all he used to do sometimes was just stare and keep staring the whole house, standing right there in the garden lawns, such was and I guess is the beauty of it.

He told me to spent my weekends here and said maybe we could talk something off, about work, and other things and family realated stuff. I almost got the essence in his voice of that desperateness to share his thoughts with someone, despite being a work-maniac, he had nothing to do on the off-days and he is not an outgoing person that much, unless it was related to work.

One day, when we were walking off in his garden lawn, a girl came and she said – " the whole exact address, "in a loud voice and just asked – "is this the right place, I am in"..? Brother replied and said "Yes". And without introducing her to me, he said to her, "you can carry on your way to the house", "my staff will show you your way around".

When I asked my Brother (Ayan), about her he said – she is the new tenant and that from now on, she will be living in this house. I asked him are you leaving?.., he said – "Of course". I couldn't be here all my life, he meant that he had work to attend Overseas and that he will be away for a good chunk of 5-6 months and it may can even take him a year. In other words, I thought he might be leaving this place and the town, and it was just his way to keep me on the hook.

I asked him, what does she do for living?..He told me she's a painter and she's very artistic in nature and and as you can think off – people like her usually seek such calm and peacefull place to practice their art out or may be, we can call it, a way of them to give their heart-out to their profession. He told me her name is 'Emma'.

Brother told me that I would be helping her in moving-in, and would be getting her familiar to the surroundings.

I was worried that how I would fare in the absence of him. I guess he also read that on my face. He patted me on my back and said – don't worry you can come and join me there. We could work together or he would find me a good Firm to do what I do. He said "you have options, you know", whenever you like to, feel free to...."

I relished his thoughts but I also knew he was not as pure in his sayings or his actions as he might appear to be. I also knew his love for me, but come a time if he had to choose between his other preferences and me, I doubt that he would choose me. He was one of those persons, which you would fail to know, the more you get to know him.

Brother went-on. I offered 'Emma' the helping hand in getting her stuff settled. I suddenly realized in a way that she was very controlling about everything around her and a very attention to details giving type of person. She just wants everything in a way that she wants them – everything at the right place – at the right times, but I supposed almost all the artists are that way.

I also realized that she used to smoke a lot, but one of the unsual thing was that normally you know, people would smoke with their second and third finger, but she used to smoke with her 'fourth' and the 'fifth' (the little) finger. I guess it was just another one of her ways to do things precisely but differently.

As much as she was a control freak with the objects and her art or profession, she also wanted control on the people around her, as if she wanted them to behave according to her. It was tricky to know her.

She just like my Brother wasn't able to cop with the place and the house that quickly, or you can say the massiveness of the house or the emptiness of the air around it. So, after settling down she called me and said - 'Virang' would you mind coming over on weekends, when you are not working – just like the way you used to do when your brother was here.

I said ok, as I also had very less friends except my work colleagues at that time, and also I missed Brother sometimes.

Once, I was there, she was showing me the paintings made by her. There was a strange enigma about all of them (paintings), almost all of them were uncompleted or you can say half finished, maybe it's just the way of looking at things differently I guess.

When I asked her about it, that why all of them are only half done or incomplete as they appeared to be..? She said – *" they are not incomplete, they are incompleted* and said - *she has not figured out the way it goes from here"*, and she was saying it by standing next to one of her paintings and pointing towards the area of the canvas from where it was left incomplete. Then she moved on to the next painting and pointing towards it, she said the same thing but a bit differently. She said – *" she don't know how this-one will end "*.

There was a kind of mysterious phenomenon in her eyes when she was saying these things.

I said to her – why don't you use some inspirations, you know read a few different things, get to know different people, watch something different and you might get knocked on by a beautiful idea or maybe vision as you people (artists') call it, and thereby you could complete these beautiful and mystic work of arts, I mean these paintings of yours.

She just gave a very subdued smile at first and then she laughed, but it was in a quite beautiful way. I have seen her like that for the first time. She took a bit of colour out from one of the boxes lying there and just touched if on my nose with her fingers and just pushed me back, like we use to do with a small kid and said – *"ohh you are just like all other of them, aren't you, all the other people would say the same thing after seeing this paintings, as you said 'Virang', you are just on point everytime I guess, aren't you".*

I smiled and replied and said –" yes maybe, I guess that's what advertisers are paid and supposed to do". "Why, was there anything wrong in my suggesstions 'Emma'.."?

She said no, you' were right in your own way, and told me that – she would rather inspire than being inspired. She said – *"What would happen to me tomorrow and where I would be, how my thoughts would shape up, how would I want people around me to treat me and the way they look at my art, it would all lead the way for deciding how these paintings end. Only I get to decide whether – this bridge in this painting or even this road in this painting goes left or right or they lead to a beautiful garden, or to a dark sunburnt forest with tall burnt wood trees and no greenry about them".*

Then pointing to one of her other paintings she said – " *the way this girl is looking at the Butterflies, I have not drawn her face, it's just the eyes, because I was neither happy nor sad, when I drew this.* So, I will decide whether she is looking at it with smile on her face or she's just sad".

I said to 'Emma' – but why she would be sad..?

She replied and said – "maybe she's jealous of the butterflies' freedom".

Then I said to 'Emma' by looking into her eyes – "but she has choosed this life for herself".

Emma replied – *"well than may be she's angry that the butterfly didn't stuck to an option like her and just kept moving from flower-to-flower and just keeps taking different essences".*

Emma was saying all this with a real venom in her voice, her eyes were red and there were if I am right, kind of tears underneath them, that I guess she had been controlling from coming out.

I said to her – "the animals have got all the time in the world to explore and look into different things, until they find what's best for them and maybe they could choose to roam like this for the eternity of their life and you know 'Emma' there is a share of human beings or you can say people too, that also prefers to live this way".

Emma said – "well not everyone has all the time in this world, 'Virang', do we..?"

She smiled and in a vigorious way picked up a black sketch and just stretched it all over a blank canvas. I stopped her and said what are you doing..?

She replied and said – *"you know Virang, the thing about incomplete paintings, is that, even if you destroy them all, it won't feel like you have lost something. All the work that you putted into it, to make it feel alive, but how could we dare to, when we can't make a large part of ourselves feel alive many times".*

She was that angry saying these all, and then she just faded and collapsed into my arms.

After a few days, I got to know that – she is suffering from a rare disease and that she has not much time left.

I also got to know, that there is a restless side to her which demands a lot of love, care and maybe an undivided attention. Along with it, all through the time that I spent with her, we were getting closer and she was becoming habitual of my presence.

I despite getting away from her, extended my visit to the house – even on some of the weekdays. I also despite knowing the sort of violent and uneased side of her behaviour and knowing that – she wants to and controls everything around her and she fickles and doesn't like it when nothing or even anything goes the way she doesn't want it to be, just like the way she was with her art, her paintings,….was not able to resist her subdued presence around me and I was getting to know something about her everyday.

I got to know that – she had a troubled past, no one appreciated her or even her works, a lot of her colleagues were also jealous of her at the art school, maybe she was different from them, she looked at things differently, she was kind of a really reserved student. I came to knew from one of my sources that even a few teachers were jealous of her and didn't treated her properly maybe because they realized – her works were superior than theirs.

She moved out from her dad's home, saying that she would get back after completing her degree, but when I meet them, I got to know that she has never visited them back and she doesn't even picks up their calls, but she do calls them once a month and tells them about her medical reports. She do tells them that everything is fine, but of course they knew everything was not the way she speaks it to be, as they do talk to doctors.

The next time I visited her, she seemed to have forgotten everything about that day. After a few weeks, I realized that I needed to get away from her in many ways, also I wasn't able to figure out, whether it was she who was developing an addiction for me and the moments that we spent together or it was me, who was getting addicted to her. I sometimes felt sympathy towards her, but sometimes I asked myself – "why was I even there, at the first place..?"

She was good to me almost all the times, but sometimes suddenly her behaviour would take a change and she would get very rigid on her perspective of things. Sometimes she would even shout at me.

I realized that with every passing week, her condition was getting worse and when I was near her, despite being those her best moments, I knew those were also the moments when she was most fragile and if anything or any of our conversations or ideas would not end the way she would want them to, that would frustrate the heck out of her. Even though I wished to, but I simply couldn't have accepted or said yes to everything she said, as many a times I used to forget that I was talking to her rather than someone else.

One day, she told me – "Virang you know – 'Emma' is not my real name".

I replied and said – "then what is it"..?

She said – she won't tell me. She said she had never told it to anyone else as well.

I said – "but why"..?

She said – "then people try to know you by your name, they would try to guess what type of a person you maybe, your choices, your astro signs and all".

I asked her if she would like to tell it to me..?...She said, not now, I don't think this is the day, the time, and the way,the surroundings – where I would tell you my real name.

I thought, she would tell it to me initially, but she didn't.

After a more couple of weeks – I knew it was time for me to leave her at her own. I probably didn't knew whether it was right for me to do so or not, but I had a gut feeling that she might get herself better and going on her own and that she might improve on herself and improve her health, but I also knew that maybe I would have been completely wrong and I needed to continue to visit her.

I might miss some of her habits that are different from everyone else that I have ever met – like the way she used to smoke, the pattern to it. The way she used to smile at me, even though she doesn't smiled a lot.

I also decided that I would keep an aye on her from every other way possible, and if the situation would demand for me to be there with her, I would try my best to be. I did what my senses told me to do and maybe I was a bit selfish, but I thought her condition was worsening due to me and that this would be for her better.

I told her that I am going to visit my Brother (Ayan) overseas and that I would be away for couple of months, as I also have some work there that I am doing in collaboration with my Brother.

She didn't said anything, she just smiled (the way she used to) and said – "Ok, if you have to go; you have to go".

I never thought, I mean I don't know, maybe I didn't wanted myself to fall for her anymore.

 I know, in every moment when I should have stayed away from her, I didn't do that, and could not resist myself from being in her surroundings, being available at her presence, but that day, i don't know what happened to me, when I saw her declining behaviour and health and how unpredictable and fragile she was when she was with me or near me, I decided to go away and disappear from her world.

 Of course, I would have kept an eye on her but, she would feel that, I ran away from her and I will not show up again, even though I told her that I would look to get back in couple of months.

I never called or told my Brother-Ayan about her, neither did I planned to tell him about whatever time I spent with Emma. I also thought hiding all these things from him might have consequences, but I still decided to let that thought go away for that moment.

The day I was leaving, she – Emma, called me and said that, she wanted to show me something. I visited the house, she took my hand and took me towards her art room, I mean, where she used to paint.

Very quickly and in a hasty manner - she lighted up her cigarette, and then said to me, look at this painting, I have a stranger living his house here, and yes, it's incomplete, because, I don't know whether he will come back or not. She said to me – "You know Virang, what's in it to draw about strangers..? I said no, I don't know. She said — "even though you don't know much or even anything about them, you can still predict there next move; at least in your paintings, you have control over them and all of a sudden, they are not that stranger anymore, you can give them names, the names of the people you know, and build or make them like other people we know; or give them different names, different characteristics, you can afford to know the way it ends.

I said to her — "do you think, I am a stranger to you..? **She pulled me towards her and by looking into my eyes [with that subdued, yet pretty smile of hers' and with those watery eyes], she said — "Don't come back".**

The next thing I remember, is that, I got a call from one of the neighbours of the house, saying to me that he had not seen 'Emma' from the last two days, normally she would water the plants in the garden's lawn and would pick-up her daily supply of flowers and articles or newspapers, but there has been no such activity at 'the house' in those two days. I immediately rushed back there.

When I got there, the main door looked like it was closed, but it wasn't, I just pushed it and it opened.

When I went in there was nobody in the hallway, I immediately rushed upstairs into the room which Emma used for her artwork.

 I saw Emma lying in the corner, she had slit her wrist. I was shivering but not from the cold, and stammering her name, I was not able to take what I saw, what the fuck has happened, I started slaping myself that it was my mistake, I should not have left her alone, I shouldn't have quitted on her, I should not have walked away from her, if I continued to visit her and persisted and stayed with her, she would have been alive.

In the middle of all these, I saw a note lying there – written in it was – *"I Want to love You More, but I Can't" - Emma*

When I picked myself up, and took a look around, **all the paintings were burnt. She had burnt all of them; just like the way she told it to me earlier – talking about burning all of them and still not feel like loosing anything or loosing them.**

There was a white canvas lying there just in behind of all those others burnt away. When I stepped close to it, in the middle of it was written that –

"Emma, that's my only and real name". "I was just testing you", "but I never thought, I would be telling it to you this way". "Maybe this is the time, surroundings, the way and the day when I tell you this".

Then I remembered, it was in the same way and those were the same things that she said to me, when I asked her real name.

It was also written there that – *"just like all of my other paintings, this one is not incomplete, and also you know 'Virang', it's different from them, that's' why I have not burnt it".*

7

VIRANG

I remember when I met her, sometimes when she smoked, I used to light it up for her. She would say – "You are not going to do it for long". I used to say – "I can do it for life-long". She would reply and say – "We will see".

Now, I came to knew that there was truth hidden in her words.

"Anna", the note which you told me about, that you found, yes, now you know Anna, that was written by 'Emma'. I cutted her name from it, as I knew that note belonged to and was written by 'Emma' for me, but I did not wanted anybody else to know about it... I thought nobody else would open that cupboard, except me...and I kept it there after "Neha" was no more, as I could not afford to loose the whole of that note, but I guess, I already lost whole of Emma.

Of Course I did told you to look after that cupboard and see if it needs a rearrangement after "Neha", as I was not able to restore the courage to look after it anymore.

Other thing of 'Emma' that is left with me is yes, that last canvas that she left me with that note. That is still there in her art room, the way she left it to me.

The girl you saw in the garden lawn Anna, I don't know who she would have been, but yes, if she was "Emma", and if she did talked to you and said the things that she did. I and you need no second guessing, but it directly hints that she wants you to be part of her story, she wants you to be in her paintings.

Maybe she wants that every character in her art..that is her world..must know the whole truth.

Maybe she's still in this house, maybe she still paints and continues to do it the way she wants everything to be.

Maybe she still controls or wants to control everything, every move, that anyone does around her.

She was just that way, and i guess she has not changed either.

But I know it deep and inside down, that she won't harm or hurt any one of us, I guess she was herself too hurt and harmed, and I wish I could have helped her more.

8

VIRANG

Pretty soon, the Brother got there. He came to knew all of that happened. We got away with the other things, as my brother's reach was good and many of the officials on the case knew him.

Also we got in touch with Emma's parents and they told the officials all about her medical history and her health and those of her sudden changes in behaviour pattern and of course, the way she was. It was indeed presumed that – she met herself to death.

But, as I told you Anna, my Brother-Ayan is not as good as a person, as he seemed to be. The news about 'Emma' quickly catched the fire and no one was willing to move into the house, there were no takers for it.

Brother, as he knew that me and Emma were spending time together as I used to tell him sometimes about her, but only the good parts.

 And I also guess some of the neighbours might also have struck his ears.

He threatened me that he would tell the officials about me and Emma, unless i take my things and move-into the house and start living there.

Both of us, my Brother-Ayan and I knew that - what was presumed about Emma's death, was true and there was no other reason for it. I had nothing to hide. But we knew – if the matter about or anything about me and Emma got out and the investigation extends, it could be tricky.

Eventhough, there were no lies to be afraid of – I couldn't take a chance with my carrier and everything else on the line. So, I decided to move into that house.

With a wicked smile – Brother told me that I need to stay here, till the air about Emma's death clears out and any presumptions in the area about the house goes away.

He said, if people will see there are persons or even a person living here – regardless of even some of them knowing that you are my brother, the house slowly and gradually will get back to its normal value, as it will be a bad idea to leave it abandoned for a period of time with no takers and buyers for it.

Everything must get back to normal and as it was before.

He doesn't knew, nor did I – what time it will take to get the things to as they were before Emma, but still he left me with no choice, other than to stick with it.

9

VIRANG

After a month, I met "Neha" at a bus stop. We chatted along and got common good vibes from each other. Our thoughts on some of the topics were quite same, we exchanged numbers. The friendship grew, we started to hang out. After a couple of weeks we started dating. Everything went well.

I decided to move-in with her. I told my Brother-Ayan about it. He was quite surprised and happy at the same time.

He said – "I thought you wanted to get away from the house, as soon as possible, I'm glad you are moving ahead with your life, and dumping all those past blemishes and memories". He said all these with a touch of arrogance.

10

When 'Neha' moved-into the house with me, we were getting to know each other even more, every day.

But, somehow I was not able to get everything that happened over the last couple of months or so, out of my system.

I felt like sometimes I saw 'Emma'. Maybe she wanted to talk to me about her paintings. I never went in that 'Art room' of hers' again. But I often used to – get to its' door, and think a bit about her ('Emma') and then leave from there.

11

I started to spend more time at work than I did with Neha. We had very little conversations and time that we spent together. Sonmehow I felt I was scared to be more with that house or to be more with Neha.

As every moment that we spent together, I felt like telling her more about all the things that happened there.

But the thought of leaving that house never appeared in my mind, I guess I never wanted to think that way or think about it.

When I think about it now, it appears to me that maybe "Emma' would have not let me to leave that house and go somewhere else.

12

The distances were growing between me and Neha. She acted a bit frustrated sometimes.

We both started to loose our cool on even small-small topics. The thought process of ours, that seemed to be so similar when we first met, seemed to be a country mile apart now.

One day, she grabbed me and said – "Virang, I want to love you more, but I can't".

I was in deep shock, as those were the exact same words, that "Emma" left me with.

Sometimes Neha also asked me – "Virang do you love someone else…,or is their anything that you want to share with me"..?

Neha said – "I want us to separate our ways and maybe give each other a bit of time for a while, but I can't leave you, I m not able to.."

She said – " I don't know why – but I just don't feel like doing it…" "I know you need me Virang.."

I knew 'Emma' would not let either me or Neha to leave that house.

She ('Emma') wants to stay near me, and maybe Neha and me staying together in the house, feels to her the best appropriate way of staying near me.

 Maybe this was the way, she would like the things to go ahead, that was the way she wanted to control things, that was the way in which she wanted the story to go ahead, in possession of every move, just like she used to do with her paintings and the way in which she described them.

13

Anna, then that office party, which I told you about-happened.

It was in the heat of all those things happening between me and Neha, and the increasing closeness between Kaya and me, Ronin caught me and Kaya in that moment of togetherness or in that weak moment of ours.

I knew he would try to destroy everything that I had, and when I managed to grab a look of him, while he was quickly trying to escape, he thought that – I had not seen him. But I do saw him.

After that, in the party I saw him typing a lot of texts in his mobile phone and, also speaking to someone for a moment or two.

My gut feeling told me that he was speaking to 'Neha', and maybe he is trying to pursue her in believing what he thinks about me, by sending her what he just captured. I saw him leaving the party. I excused everyone else and left after him.

I assumed, whatever he (Ronin) told Neha over the text and in their conversation, and even if he sent that picture of me and Kaya to her, either it was not proving enough for Neha to believe Ronin, or she must have reacted in such a way that Ronin wanted to show her those himself, and also maybe the other instances of me and Kaya together at the work or at some other places.

14

The next thing I remember is seeing – two cars in the middle of the road, in that dark snowy winter's night.

It seemed to me like, both the cars crashed into each other with speed and then stopped at a fair distance from each other.

There were sparks flying out of one of the cars, it seemed like everything has happened just a moment ago before I got there. There was no one else other around at that time.

I recognized both of the cars, I slowly stepped out of my car, and went towards one of them, my heart was beating very fast. When I got there, the car's front mirror was covered with snow, I wiped it with my hands, and I saw 'Neha' lying in her front driving seat with her head held back and her eyes closed, there was blood coming out of her head also. I checked her pulse, there was nothing there. She was gone. I was so out of my mind. I started to sob and cry her name again and again, but there was not moment from her. The next thing I remember is, when I walked a few steps and got to the other car, it was Ronin's car. He was tilted out of his driving seat and half fallen into the road. There was his mobile phone-just a fair distance away from his hands. And yes, there was that picture of me and Kaya, that he took at the party and underneath that there were texts messages, all sented to Neha.

I don't know, I was just so angry, I felt this whole thing has happened because of him. Whatever has happened to Neha is because of him. Maybe I knew – I was also to blame for it, if I did not have gotten closer to Kaya at the party and what happened between us, shouldn't have happened; then Ronin wouldn't have seen us. All this will never have happened.

15

I went back to my car, and with an uncalculated enigma of anger in my head, I hitted Ronin with my car. I sat there in my driving seat, and I was shivering with anger at the same time, holding my steering wheel. I never thought I was capable of this kind of brutality, even for the one's – that I cared for and loved.

As I was sitting in my car, a car came and probably in that snowy night and with all the less visibility on offer, it took the bended turn on the road and hitted Neha's car from the side, which was facing that turn. That car left after stopping for about a minute, and after seeing that there were three cars there, all pretty messed up, except mine's. So, I got my head down on my steering wheel, thinking about all the things happened.

As soon as that car left, and I was going back to Neha's car, there was a massive explosion and blast – Neha's car was blown all over.

I just couldn't process the fact that – despite being with her and looking at her in her perhaps the last moments with me, I decided to do what I did with Ronin.

I shouted at the open skies – "no, you can't do that to me, you can't take away everything from me".

16

In The Present

ANNA

(Comes near the dejected Virang) and consoles him and says – "you did what u did in complete rage. Sometimes, we don't know what we are doing (Anna hugs Virang). You did it because it was 'Neha' that you lost. Maybe you never thought of loosing her, and that too in that way in which you lost her.

VIRANG

(Walks a little) and says – "no, no, no; how could I" (with his face facing down, and not being able to meet his eyes with Anna).

ANNA

(Asks Virang) "Virang is their anything else you want to tell me, why you seem like you want to tell me something, but you are hiding it at the same time"…? (Anna grabs Virang by his chin and says look at me, while sobbing) and says – please tell me, (shouts), tell me Virang.

VIRANG

Anna, "when I hit Ronin with my car – (stammers) he..he…." (Anna says – " he what..? say it Virang").

"He was alive". I came to knew it, but still I did that.

ANNA

Slowly walks away from Virang and sits on one of the chairs. Holds her head with both of her hands in an inconsolable shock and starts to cry.

VIRANG

(Comes near Anna) and keeps his hand on her shoulder and says - Anna, (but Anna slowly removes it) and walks away.

17

After 4 Months

Virang is standing outside a bookstore. Anna is the guest author – signing some of her books for her readers and followers. Virang walks-in the store, with one of Anna's books in his hand and stands right at the end of the line, rather secretively.

When his turn comes, and he moves ahead and Anna gets her head up and asks for the book, she recognizes him (Virang). Virang looks at her with a bit of smile. But Anna stands up, takes her stuff and walks away from the store.

Virang follows her for a bit, but doesn't says anything or not even shouts her name, and then stops and let Anna leave.

Virang takes out a cigarette, lights it up (and while smoking) he thinks about this --

(on the next page)

18

Flashback (from the night of the accident)

Virang, after hitting Ronin with his car, backs his car away, and with full speed rushes towards Neha's car and hits it from the side, and then again backs his car away and rushes towards Neha's car and again hits it, but this time from the front.

Virang then drives away with his car from the scene and stops after a fair distance. He then takes out a cigarette from one of the front boxes of his car, lights it up and starts to smoke.

He is holding the cigarette with his 'fourth' and the 'fifth' (the little) finger; (the way "Emma" used to hold it)..and continues to smoke that way.

He then throws the cigarette away, starts the car, and goes away.

Notes

ACKNOWLEDGEMENT

I would like to express my special thanks of gratitude to all those people around me, who believed in me during the process of writing this Novel. There's a saying – "you can buy things with wealth, but you can't buy a friend or people that support you.

In this modern world, nothing is a big achievement, as in Hindi – we use to say – "to kya hua". But I think if you do your work with right intentions and deliver the content that you want to deliver to your segment of audience and manage to do it with subtle honesty. There is a sense of inner achievement attached to it, and if we can build on that, we can grow and become good human beings.

The audience's feedback is my food. Sometimes, I will get the bad ones as well, but that's the part of my job, and I will try my best that next time I turn them into good ones.

Thanks to all the people who gave a chance to this stuff [I promise I won't disappoint you].

(By the way)

"Sometimes a piece of paper can understand your thoughts better than those around you" – M.K

"Maybe she was an art...

that fades away from the canvas...

but never fades away

from your mind and your heart"...